CW00840065

MEMOIRS OF A BREAD MAN

JUSTIN JOHN SCHECK

Published 2020 by Magnum Opus – A Next Chapter Imprint

Edited by Tyler Colins

Cover art by Cover Mint

ACKNOWLEDGMENTS

I'd like to thank my Father first and foremost, as he was the inspiration for writing this novella. He is the reason I set out to write it in the first place, to examine our relationship and hopefully become a better man as he would want in the process. I'd also like to thank my Mother and Bro and Sis for always being there for me. Finally I'd like to thank my friends Jim Johnson and David Polsky who helped me revise and edit *Memoirs of a Bread Man* when I first completed it, as well as Next Chapter for finalizing it with me.

PREFACE

In 2008 I found myself somewhere I had never been before. I was working at a hospital in Chicago, Illinois when my world was completely turned upside down. An overwhelming fear overtook me as I had suffered a major psychotic break and was later diagnosed with schizoaffective disorder.

I was living with four close friends that had become strangers to me as my reality shifted and, for some reason at this confusing and life altering juncture in my life, all I could think to do was write. I had three years prior moved to Chicago from Madison, Wisconsin where I had worked as a bread man, and I chose my last days in that world, centered around Christmas 2004, as my subject matter. It was a Christmas unlike any other as I discovered, as my father recently had, that he had been exposed to Agent Orange all those years ago in Vietnam, and that he now had cancer.

I wrote to analyze what has and had happened to me—a therapy novella if you will. I wanted to examine the early signs of my illness and the way my father shaped my life, and the lens through which I saw things then and at the present time. So, on a couch with a laptop I sat and spent four months writing what would become *Memoirs of a Bread Man*.

INTRODUCTION

So, what might one glean from a reading of *Memoirs of a Bread Man*? What is it to be a Bread Man? What are the effects of war on humanity? What do the early stages of a creeping mental illness look and feel like? What is manic love in its worst form? The answers to these questions aren't what I set out to answer in this novella; they are simply the reality of who it is that I am. The reader will get a glimpse of these things as I tell my story … a story about bread. A blue-collar diary.

Christmas Eve 2004 my father called to tell me that he had cancer. He had contracted Agent Orange nearly forty years prior in Vietnam, and cancer had come to my family while I was a state away, still trying to find myself. I was twenty-five and delivering and selling bread in Madison, Wisconsin with no clue what I was doing there. My mother and father still lived outside of Chicago where I had gone to high school, and I was bouncing around the Midwest working odd jobs, reading Kerouac and waiting for God to lead me to my destiny. I knew it wasn't being a Bread Man, but I had accumulated so much debt from undiagnosed manic states that I got stuck, so to speak, and it was the best paying job I could find not having a degree.

My relationship with my boss, "Frankie", an ex-Master Gunnery

Marine Drill Sergeant kept me on the job. I considered it my duty to look out for him, being a vet and all. My father would have wanted me to, and he needed all the help he could get. I stayed on longer than I wanted to because I saw my father in him. They both had severe PTSD; both had served in combat and both looked after me.

I was trying to help "Frankie" keep his job as his new boss was gunning for him and the job was all that "Frankie" had. If it were up to me, I would have been in L.A. trying my luck as a musician—which I would actually do later that summer—instead having moved to Chicago, where I would quite rapidly descend into full-blown schizoaffective disorder. Unbeknownst to me, I had always been bipolar and had PTSD, and our story takes place during a descent into a depressed episode. Yes, all these things are part of this novella, but that's not what this novella is about.

This novella became a process for me to analyze my relationship with my father, and how his life decisions, especially his decision to go to Vietnam instead of college, ended up shaping my life forever.

PROLOGUE

THE EARLIEST MEMORY I HAVE OF MY FATHER IS OF HIM teaching me how to frisk a man. His shoulders blocked what later I knew were palms pressed firmly against a granite wall, arms outstretched, feet spread wider than his shoulders.

He was in his underwear and had on a pair of grey tube socks with three red stripes at the top. Years later I remembered him wearing an aqua blue T-shirt, but I can't be sure anymore.

He told me to sit on the couch with my eyes closed and wait until he hid the weapon.

"O.K. Now open your eyes and frisk me," he said.

I instantly spotted the long screwdriver awkwardly sticking out of his right sock. I was seven.

I walked right over to him, bent down, and grabbed the handle with my right hand.

"Stop," he ordered. "Slowly turn your head up to the left." Just above me was a knife, held and cocked.

"Always start at the top," he said.

PART 1

1

IT'S THREE A.M. IN MADISON, WISCONSIN, LATE DECEMBER 2004.

"Let me tell you somethin', Junior."

My boss, Frankie, is in early to train a new guy today. He is an Old School Bread Man, now the District Sales Manager of the least-grossing division in the Midwest. He often refers to himself as a midget (he's about 5'8") but everything else about him is huge—not in muscle, but in his Drill Sergeant voice and wild eyes. He stares straight into me, his face tilted slightly downwards, adjusts his hat and says, "Let me explain something to you, O.K.? This is how it works. Women go crazy at thirty-five. They have their mid-life crisis at thirty-five. When *we* have our mid-life crisis, we buy sports cars and drink our faces off. Women go crazy, tell you they never loved you, and have some twenty-something lawyer—still happily married 'cause his wife hasn't snapped yet—hand you divorce papers at a Stop-N-Go gas station on the south side of Milwaukee. You'll say to yourself I didn't even know we were fighting. But she's unhappy and that's that."

He pauses to take a breath, breathing in deeply and then violently out his nose. "Now, you'll find yourself walking out the front door with a red suitcase in your hand, your wife, house, and children to your back, wondering when you're gonna be on 'Americas Most Wanted', 'cause in her mind you're a goddamn criminal. That time you were drivin' and your eight-year-old daughter started kicking you in the head and calling you a fucker, and you grabbed her by the shirt and threw her in the back seat—that was child abuse. Or that time you begged your wife for sex 'cause it had been eight months, and she finally gave in—that was rape. When she was thirty-four, you were a father and a husband. Now that she's thirty-five, you're a child abusing rapist."

Again, he breathes loudly. It sounds like a punctuation mark before his words again race past. "So there you are in front of a judge—a child-abusing rapist—and he's looking at you like all you've done for the past twenty years was drink beer and watch professional wrestling. He doesn't know that you've been getting up at two in the fuckin' morning to deliver bread since your first child was born so you could be home at noon to raise your kids while the wife goes off to her five-fifty-an-hour job cause she has friends there and she likes to get out of the house. He doesn't know it was you changing the diapers, watching a dancing purple dinosaur sing the same goddamn song for the ten millionth time, fixing lunch and dinner, picking the kids up from school and band practice, their friends' houses … nor does he know that by the time she gets home you've been up for fifteen hours and you've spent the last fourteen years trying to function on two hours of sleep. He doesn't know that she's been fucking your best friend for the past eight months, and you don't either, not yet anyway. He doesn't know and he doesn't care, cause he's seventy goddamn years old, and when his wife was thirty-five it was the 1940s, and leaving the prick wasn't an option."

Still staring through me he says, "Eventually, this mother fucker tells you that she gets half. You know what 'half' means, boy? It means *all* of it. She gets the kids 'cause she's the mother. Since she gets the kids, she gets the house, 'cause the kids need a place to stay. She gets what's left in the bank account 'cause she'll need it to pay for the house and the babysitter while she's off at the bar with her new single friends pretending she's twenty again. She'll need the babysitter 'cause the children can't be left alone with a child-abusing rapist. You'll hear that your best friend is living in your house, fuckin' your wife, raising your children, living on your money 'cause they won't marry. Soon, you'll be living under a bridge sleeping next to black feet, cause if you're not workin' all she gets half of is nothin'. Eventually, you'll come to what's left of your senses and get back on a route, living on baloney sandwiches because it's all you can afford—that and the Jameson you'll need to keep you from shooting yourself in the face and jumping in the fuckin' river."

Sitting on the bumper of a bread truck, surrounded by bread and the stench of the depot, I listen carefully and think to myself my boss is both crazy and immaculately sane at the same time. I say "carefully" because I don't want my face to show anything. He is an ex-Master Gunnery Marine Drill Sergeant and he generally knows what you're thinking before you do. Even if he doesn't, it won't matter. Once he's sure, he's sure. I've learned not to argue. If it's in his head, it's true. After two months of him yelling at me, I eventually realized it was because he liked me.

Kim, a forty-something Bread Vet, has been standing at Frankie's side throughout the monologue, holding up his hands, palms facing me, calmly smiling and nodding in agreement as though Frankie were a preacher. His approach is much more relaxed, the pacing of his Muppet voice much more careful.

"He's right," Kim nods. "See, sometimes they don't leave you though. But you'll wish they had. My wife was always crazy. But it wasn't till thirty-five that the … the goal of my marriage changed. See, you have to understand that women's brains are made differently. She was always crazy, but at thirty-five my vows became, no matter what, that I will not kill her."

He smiles and grabs his belly, round like Santa Claus' in my younger mind's eyes, as Frankie lights up a menthol and starts bitching about the new guy being late.

"See, that's how you'll spend the rest of your life, day in and day out, trying not to kill her," Kim states.

He's smiling at you, somehow looking both serious and amused.

"Where the fuck is this guy, Junior?" Frankie growls at me.

"If he's smart, he's asleep," answers Walter.

"It's almost three fuckin' thirty in the goddamn morning! I don't have time for this."

"What time did you tell him to be here?" I ask.

"Four a.m. What the fuck are you doing here on time anyway, boy? You sick or something?"

"I couldn't sleep."

"Couldn't sleep! What do ya think, Walt?"

Frankie starts circling his lighter in an upside-down fist over an imaginary bong and adds, "Is that code for I got drunk and stoned all night, and decided to come to work 'cause if I went to sleep I'd never get up? What do ya think, boys?"

Walter clears his throat, and says in his deep voice, "He was probably ..."

"Where the fuck is this guy, Junior!" Frankie interrupts. All of Frankie's questions are rhetorical. He has no interest in your response.

He's getting more anxious now. He starts breathing heavily, snorting and wheezing, and rubbing his hand back and forth atop his crew cut, the other hand holding his baseball cap by the brim. He makes the sounds of a nose cleaned out by coke, and the huffing from lungs coated with Marlboro Menthol.

Your first day on the job—Walter explained—if you wanted any sort of life while being a Bread Man, you'd carry an eight ball on you at all times. "You'll need it if you ever want to see your friends again," he had said.

Walter has been a Bread Man for twenty-one years. He has no friends left.

2

WE MOVED TO ANOTHER PART OF NORTHEAST OHIO RIGHT before I entered the third grade. No more rummaging through the bike and car graveyard in back of my best friend Tommy's house in Brunswick, fishing for spare parts to build go-karts, a new bike to crash, or to get a moped running while Tommy's father was off either working or hunting with his coon dogs.

Ohio is a strange place. There is, of course, Cleveland—the core—and then there are the suburbs; but the periphery, the rural areas, are more deep south than mid-west. And Brunswick was a dichotomy of both the suburbs and the rural areas of Ohio. We no longer lived in the rural part of Brunswick, rather right along the border of the suburbs. I was too young for it to be a culture shock. I was eight or nine in my memory. It was sometime in the 80s, right after that teacher died on the space shuttle that blew soon after lift-off.

I remember because my brother—a fifth grader—was sent home for saying, "People die every day. Why should we care just 'cause it's on TV?"

According to his home room teacher, he was "void of sympathy and emotion, and should go home and think about what he had said."

Obviously, she had never frisked a man.

I had an awful time adjusting, suffering panic attacks constantly, though I and no one else seemed to know that is what was happening to me at the time. Three months into school, they assigned me a friend. They called it "the buddy system".

My teacher sent me into the hall, and when she came to get me, she said I'd be sitting at a new desk, next to my new friend, Jeff Idle.

Poor bastard must have raised his hand when she asked for a volunteer. It's a task no adult would accept. These things require the bravery of innocence.

I instantly took to following him everywhere he went. I followed him out of the classroom, into the bathroom, back into the hall, outside school, all over the playground, and so on. The crying spells and panic attacks stopped, and I felt safe.

I remember him looking over his shoulder at me, blue eyes widening. At first, he was reticent, perhaps regretting his decision, but soon we became best of friends, which led to more friends.

We moved again five years later—my freshman year of high school —this time two states away to Illinois.

3

RING ... RING ... RING.

“Just a minute, I got to put my ear in. Hello?"

"Hey Pop, how ya doin’?"

"Hi son! Good, good. You know. Just sittin' in ma' chair, watching some stupid movie. How you doin'? You need any money or anything?"

"No, I’m good, Pop."

“Thanks for callin’ me, son.”

I’d just stepped outside to give my dad a call. He’s up at random, and I’ve caught him four hours before he has to go to work.

"Life is runnin’ me ragged, goin' everywhere. I mean, I gotta go in early all week to set up the gymnasium for the volleyball practices, then drive out to Rockford, to the VA, cause I gotta see the doctor ‘bout my feet. Man, I don't get a second to rest—I’m tellin' ya."

After my father had taken early retirement from 3M—a buy-out that he couldn't refuse at the time—he discovered rather quickly that health care costs would bleed his pension dry by the time he turned sixty-five, so he started working again, this time at my old high school as a janitor and a Saint.

I'm sure his new boss had realized by now that he tends to be concentrating on five things at once. No more, no less.

There's nothing you could possibly do or say that wouldn't tie his mind to a memory, which would then tie to another, until there were five realities circling behind his eyes, all serving the jungles of Vietnam.

"You just startin' workin'?" he asks.

"Yeah. I just got here. How's Mom?"

"She's good. She's upstairs sleepin'. So ..."

"Good. Is she getting much rest lately?"

"You know your mother. She tosses and turns and tosses. Hell, my farts wake her up!" He starts to laugh in that familiar high-pitched squeal. "Then I gotta hear about it the next day," he says as he laughs —bellows really. "I'm tellin' ya. You know what I mean?"

"Your farts wake her up?" I ask, laughing.

"Yeah!" he yells. "Boy, do I hear it. How you sleepin'? You got tough hours, man."

"Hey. I'm sorry Pop, but I gotta get going. I've got to get back to work. Love you," I stress.

"O.K. Love you, too."

I pull the phone down and hear him start chewing on what sounds like potato chips before I hang up and walk back into the front door of the depot.

4

It's four a.m. The new guy walks in, one eye open, and Frankie starts immediately. "You're late!"

He checks his watch, tilting his head to the side, looking almost around his glasses. "Lets see ... why it's four o'clock on the dot," he states.

"You ain't no Bread Man. Bread Men come half an hour early to check everything. You never know what's gonna go wrong. Now, load the fuckin' truck," orders Frankie.

The new guy smiles.

"That is true. You never know what's gonna go wrong, that's for sure, ain't it?" he laughs.

I say hello and introduce myself. I shake his hand and discover that his name is Harold. He's an Old School Bread Man, but much kinder. "Old School Bread Man" usually means the kind of Bread Man that'll smash all your loaves and throw them in a cart in the back room if you steal one loaf of space on their shelf. The kind of Bread Man that'll take a bobby pin, heat it with a lighter, and singe all your bags, leaving the tiniest of holes, "stalein" out your bread. Harold is not that kind of man I'll come to find, but is someone who somehow survived that era.

He's in his early forties I decide, but he looks younger. This would make it his third time with the company. Frankie's' new boss Todd had hired him.

Todd was out of Chicago—a thirty-something alcoholic cokehead Mormon with a sports car and a coked-out wife currently in rehab. He was brought in to turn the District around. Since Todd had done the hiring, poor Harold never had a chance.

"What is this? Like your thirteenth time with the company there, Harold? How the hell are you not blacklisted yet? You better not be wastin' my time."

This time, Harold doesn't laugh.

We all get back to loading our trucks. It's Monday, so there's no doubt there'll be a lot of stale bread to take off the shelves. It's going to be a long day.

5

THE WINTERS IN MADISON, WISCONSIN BRING WITH THEM all the ghosts and regrets of a lifetime. Pale blue winter ice brings gifts if seen through the proper lens, and curses if you haven't properly squeegeed that third eye. This particular winter brought thoughts of love.

The Cold hates. It cuts through to the bones, freezes everything but the heart.

Maybe it was Natalie who started this particular domino. She worked at the coffee shop next to where I lived, and something about her reminded me of love. I would sometimes go into the shop to write, and I'd find myself scanning the counter just to watch her every time I looked up.

It was a subtle draw at first, hoping that as the line shortened, she'd be the one in the rotation to take my order. I didn't admit this to myself right away, or maybe just didn't notice, having so much on my mind.

I was writing some shitty poems, just writing and writing as an exercise, five or six cups of dark-roast coffee into the day, when I glanced over and saw what looked like dancing. She was simply stirring a cup of freshly poured coffee. Her face held no expression when she lifted it to her lips, softly blowing, and then stretching to meet the rim of the mug. She was beautiful.

I stopped thinking. I didn't say anything to myself. I had already closed my notebook, and was walking towards the counter, empty-headed, calm, like a picture of myself in my head. “Hi,” I greet.

She smiles and says, “Hello.”

I tell her my name followed with, “I don't mean to be forward, but I've been hoping to somehow strike up a conversation with you, and in this environment that doesn't seem to be possible, you being so busy and all. Please know that I'm sincere in saying I would love, *love,* to get to know you better, and I'm hoping you've found yourself curious about me, too. Can I buy you lunch if you're not busy after work? I hear the place across the street is nice. Have you ever been?.”

She smiles brightly and looks up, her rising eyes rolling slowly to the left. “No I haven't actually. I'd like that,” she says.

I still have no recollection of what happened next, but three hours later she was meeting me at a restaurant across the street.

She sat and said she'd have the same, a Guinness, as we looked over the menus.

It had been almost three years since I sat across the table from a girl at a restaurant.

"Just so you know, I’m kinda, sorta involved right now ... just so you know," she tells me.

6

DID I MENTION THAT I CAN'T EAT CAKE?

Some time, early on, when I was six or seven, at the end of dinner on Thanksgiving or Christmas, my grandmother—my father's mother—asked in her low gravelly voice, "Why isn't anyone eatin' my cake? I made all this cake and now no one's eatin' it."

She was holding the cake at her waist, a cigarette hanging out of her mouth. As a child she had gotten polio and, ever since, couldn't get her hand on her right arm above her hips. She set the cake down as she finished her violent and absurd dialogue.

My brother—always the bravest of the lot—got up from the table of aunts and uncles, sons and daughters, and daughters-in-law, brothers and sisters and cousins. He made his way over to the long school lunch table where all the food sat, and grabbed a slice of cake.

Her response was, "You don't need any more, fat boy."

The turning of the tables, my father screaming in the jungle, my uncles holding him back by grabbing him by the arms, hands sliding from chest to throat. Later that night my Uncle Kenny would slash my Uncle Al in the arm with a steak knife over the last piece of that very cake. What remains is that I can't eat cake.

I bring this up because it's Walter's twenty-first year as a Bread

Man. He's about to marry for the fourth time—a woman he refers to as "number four"—and she and "the kid" have baked him an anniversary cake that he has brought in to share. Frankie and Harold and Kim have all gathered and as Frankie starts to slice it, I close the back door of the truck and step up into the front.

"Aren't you going to have any cake, boy? You look like shit. You should eat something," says Frankie.

"I already ate," I reply. The cake has knocked the wind out of me, and my thoughts drift back to Ohio.

7

THE THING ABOUT A MEMORY IS THE WAY IT COMES AND goes. A man has ample time to think when he's on a bread route. The mind wanders when it gets behind the wheel.

I remember, in third grade, Sophia kicking wood chips on the playground at recess, waiting for her friend to walk over and ask me if I liked Sophia or if I liked her liked her."

I remember a workbench in the basement of our first house in Ohio where I would use my father's tools just to feel more like him.

I remember a round blue suitcase, but not the trip.

I remember that my first love's hair was dyed red, that she wore black Converse, and that her eyes changed from green to blue and back again in the little while that I knew her.

I remember holding my brother's glasses after school in the park when he fought Thomas LaGrange.

I remember the way I would *un*-focus my eyes ... the wind gusting, then whispering, then drifting off around the side garage in autumn while I stared at the metal fence in the backyard.

I remember my father could make me hyperventilate with the loudness of his voice until I was far older than I care to admit.

I remember what happened early on in our new home, when my father contemplated murder in the place my parents live still, a small farming town in Illinois.

8

Love haunted me all winter long, and I would dream of Natalie when I slept. I would envisage waking up with her in my bed. I dreamed of her in a wedding dress. I would think about her while stopped at red lights, strapping stacks of shells of bread to the walls of a bread truck. I would think of her while picking orders in the morning, writing orders at the end of the day, while speaking to Store Managers and Back-Room Receivers. I would think of her while sipping coffee and smoking cigarettes.

Since I've yet to know her, I can think of nothing else.

9

It's four-thirty a.m. and I'm on my way to my first account. I'm driving atop slush and ice in what Frankie calls a "coffin on wheels", namely, a bread truck. It's a big box, like a UPS truck, so lightweight that a good wind could blow you off course, and since we were the least-grossing division of Butternut Bread in the Midwest, the coffin was lighter than normal. Our truck upkeep was far less than adequate, and we slid around with no heat, no air-conditioning, and frequent breakdowns.

My phone rings and I struggle to answer it, fishing around in my pocket, one hand on the wheel.

"Yeah," I say quickly.

"Yeah! What the fuck kinda way is that to answer the phone boy? Yeah?" demands Frankie.

There is silence and I realize that he's not going to say anything until I say hello.

"Hello!" I shout.

"Yeah, ah. No one's dying on my watch. Todd can go fuck himself. If we were overseas, I'd'a fragged his ass on day one."

"So, what's up, Frankie?"

“Yeah, I uh, just wanted to let you know that if the roads are too slick, then bring ‘er in. O.K.”

“Alright,” I say.

“Alright, Junior, that’s all I got for now.”

I hang up and glance down to see that my tank is on “E”. I’m late, but I’m practically running on fumes. I pull off the highway into a gas station the first chance I get. I hop out, quickly grab the nozzle, and check the time.

Everything about the job takes five or ten minutes, and if you’re not careful, it can add up to twelve- or fourteen-hour days.

I run in and grab a cup of coffee, add cream, skip stirring, grab a pack of Lucky non-filters, pay the man, and away I go. Only when I try to return the gas nozzle to put the company card in and pay, I notice something strange. The diesel already has a nozzle in its holder. Only the 87 unleaded is open. I just filled a diesel truck to the brim with gasoline. I hadn’t made one delivery, and my day was already over.

Ring … ring … ring.

“Yeah?”

“Ah, Frankie,” I try to say calmly.

"Yeah?”

“I just fucked up pretty bad.”

“What’s wrong, boy?”

“Well, I just filled up the truck…”

“It won’t start?”

“I filled it with regular gasoline.”

I close my eyes and brace for the blow.

He begins to laugh, slowly and sparsely at first, then builds into a crescendo, and into belly laughter. “Go home,” he says sharply.

“I haven’t even done …”

“Adams, be a Bread Man. Take all the bread and throw it in the nearest dumpster, call a tow truck, then go home and drink your face off. And don’t worry about Todd, ‘cause we got shorted all your bread today, right?

Good. O.K.”

10

NATALIE WAS FIVE YEARS YOUNGER THAN ME AND A biology major at The University of Wisconsin. She later told me that she fell in and out of love with me three times in the first two weeks, and that the other guy she was "kinda' sorta' seein'" was blowing her off until he heard about me. The confusion she said spawned from the fact that he seemed safer—me being what her father would later refer to as a bohemian.

"He's a bohemian. He'd be good for you," he would say.

The third time she broke it off with me, something about my heart changed. So, when she ended it with the other guy for good, and gave her heart to me, I had already begun to grow a bit numb.

I remember walking with her up and down the hilly road by her apartment, near campus, past long rows of trees and houses soon after we'd first met. This is when she told me how her mother just up and left one day when she was a little girl. We sat near a park, atop huge concrete blocks, and talked. She told me that I scared her, and that she was afraid I would just up and leave too. I couldn't reassure her, so I kissed her instead.

11

SOON AFTER WE MOVED TO ILLINOIS, MY FATHER mentioned ...

"If anything ever happens to your mother, I'm gonna burn that S.O.B. alive for what he does to people. I'll cover him with gasoline and light a match. He's what's wrong with this world. I'll light up a cigarette tomorrow, grab my shotgun, and see to it that all those who've done wrong pay for it! An eye for an eye, and a tooth for a tooth. I'll see to it he never steals from anyone again. That son of a bitch don't know who he's dealin' with. I been dreamin' 'bout it."

My dad, forced to move his family from Ohio to Illinois when the 3M plant closed in Cleveland—and on a mere few months notice—would have to transfer, return to starting pay, and go back to the night shift.

We were living in a hotel while our house was being built, me starting my freshman year of high school and my brother his senior year. The builder, the aforementioned "S.O.B."—the one my father wants to burn alive—said he needed an extra so-and-so tens of thousands of dollars to finish the job or we'd lose the house. Coincidentally, this happened to everyone on the block.

"Mismanagement of Funds" it's called. My parents were told that they couldn't sue him for anything because everything, including his business, was in his brother's name.

My father handed over what little savings he and my mom had for fear of losing what they'd already put in. He did not unravel.

12

After waiting for hours for the tow truck, and having dumped all the bread in the dumpster behind the gas station, I get back to the depot. I get a ride in a giant machine that looks like something from one of those Monster Truck Rallies. It's designed to tow large vehicles. It's about ten a.m. and Walter is done, back already, unloading his truck.

"They haven't even fuckin' salted yet," he grouses.

A long pause.

"Where's your truck?"

I tell him what happened and he smiles his crooked smile, his top teeth shooting out from underneath his mustache in every possible direction. Walter reaches into his lunch pail and pulls out a bag of weed.

He's about 6'4, 250-some pounds. His voice is deep and his gait is pinched by a bad back and sore knees. He once told me that he had trained with the Navy Seals, that he was a demolitions expert. He also once told me that he crushed his drill sergeant's car in boot camp, when the sergeant was in it, using only his mind. To say that he's delusional would be an understatement.

"They had to get the Jaws of Life to pry him out," he had said.

Thirty minutes later we find ourselves drunk, stoned, and in the midst of a coke binge at the bar down the street.

"You're a messy boy," he says as he wipes cocaine from my nose.

"I've never done cocaine before," I admit. "We can really do this right here?"

"As long as we share" he smiles. "I've been doing coke since I got back from 'nam."

"My father served too. Two tours. He volunteered," I say.

"He volunteered! A real yahoo, huh?"

"He believed in what he was doing. Did you?"

"Fuck no. I was drafted. Though mostly I just ran drugs. Heroin. We'd load up a chopper and fly it out. I don't fuck with heroin too often anymore. That's a young man's drug. You ever do heroin?"

"Never. Never will. I'd like it too much. I can't feel my face," I say as I poke at the side of my nose and cheeks.

"Well, you got something in there," he smiles brightly. "Jerry! Your turn!" he yells under his breath.

The place is empty and Jerry—the bartender—walks over, grinning ear to ear. He does a line and howls as he stands, breathing in and pinching his nose in rhythm.

"This is Adams," says Walter.

Jerry grips my hand tightly, and I grip it back.

"So, what's your story Adams?" he asks.

"I was born out of nothingness, billions of years ago," I respond.

"Adams had a short day," Walter says as he does a line.

I retell the story as Jerry listens and laughs.

"First time he's ever been back on time," Walter tells him.

"How do you get done so fuckin' early man?" I turn and ask Walter.

"I just roll the bread in back and I have someone else stock it for me."

"Someone else stock it for you? How do you manage that?"

"I have kids in every store who stock it for me. Baggers and cashiers. I just throw them a dime of good bud every now and again."

"Really? That's brilliant," I say, astounded.

"Yeah. Pick up stale twice a week and they do the rest. I stay up $50,000, spend a few thousand on green, twenty stops. Work smarter, not harder."

"So, you just deliver the bread? That's crazy. I've been pullin' four to four everyday. I'm fucking exhausted. I barely sleep."

"Your turn." He hands me the rolled up twenty.

"I'm good, I think. I always wanted to try it, but it's making me too wound up. I don't think it's my thing."

"Suit yourself. You'll never have a life without it." He does the line for me.

"Your turn, Jerry."

I don't reiterate to him that I already don't sleep. That I have more time than I can handle.

"Fuck, yeah!" Jerry exclaims.

"I'll be right back," I say.

"You want another beam and water?" Jerry asks.

"Please." I walk out the door and call Frankie, and ask where he is.

"Jesus Christ, Junior, this fuckin' guy. I've been in two wars and I was a cop in Milwaukee for ten years, and I've never feared for my life as much as I have today. I swear I saw his eyes close three fuckin' times while he's driven the truck. I called Todd and told him, 'Why the fuck did you even hire this guy? I'm just gonna get a call in a week sayin' there's bread all over the highway and Harold is dead.' Then, I'm gonna be back on a route. Oh, I bet Todd would love that! Why do I even get up in the morning? Hold on, boy. *What?*"

There's a short pause and I hear Harold in the background.

"Alright, I got to go; Harold just got us kicked out of a Piggly Wiggly."

He leaves his cell on and I hear him yell, "Don't worry about it, Harold ... that Receivers an asshole. I'll take care of it."

I hang up, walk back inside, and notice that every muscle in me is screaming to be larger. Tighter. With eyes like saucers, I make my way back to the bar and sit down beside Walter.

At some point he starts talking about women and I confide in him about Natalie.

"I was with a girl like that once. She was squirming around and everything, so I flipped her over and stuck it in her ass. She just went wild."

There is a long pause.

"Why do you refer to your fiancée as number four?" I ask.

"'Cause she is number four. She's fat and ugly just like me. It works."

"No, I mean, what's her name?"

His face softens. "Rose."

13

MY FATHER TOLD ME ABOUT THE BIRDS AND THE BEES when I was eleven.

"You see, son, women were born out of nothingness billions of years ago, and that makes them angels. The measure of a man is how he treats angels."

That was all he said. I'm in a world I don't understand. I mean I understand the guys; I'm just different than them. They all seem to hate women or, if not, they have a boys' mentality about how to treat women, how to feel about women, and talk about women.

Natalie still made me mad with curiosity, overwhelmed by existence. The thought of love drove me, but I knew she wasn't for me. She wasn't even real, really. I can barely remember anything she has said. But if you'd ask me if I love her, I'd say yes, because I know, at the time, we need each other.

14

IT'S TWO P.M. AND WALTER GIVES ME A RIDE BACK TO THE depot. Frankie and Harold are in the front office, Frankie with a cigarette hanging out of his mouth. He's standing over Harold, who's sitting at Frankie's desk. Harold continuously keeps leaning back in Frankie's chair, knocking the phone that's on the wall off the hook. Frankie puts it back every time, all the while ranting.

"Look, Harold, the bottom line is that there's money to be made on this route, but we haven't had anyone in a while who has taken care of the stores. Like that asshole Jeff. He's not a bad guy. He's just an asshole. I sympathize with the guy."

Frankie goes on for another ten minutes about how great the route can be, and finally Harold responds with, "Say, ah, is there anywhere to get a drink around here?"

Harold sounds like a younger Robert Duvall.

Frankie looks defeated. Quietly, he asks, "Why do I even get up in the morning?"

"Sure," I say to Harold.

Five minutes later I stumble into the bar behind Harold. "Hey, Jerry!" I yell, arms held wide.

"Adams! What can I get you?"

I ask Harold what he wants.

"Let' s see ... I'll have a brandy and Coke. Thanks."

We grab a seat at a table away from the bar, and Harold sits down. I stay at the bar and wait for Jerry to pour the drinks.

I bring them over to the table and light a cigarette. "So, whadya think of old Frankie so far?"

"He's pretty crazy," he says, laughing. "You shoulda seen him lay into the Receiver at the last stop, the Piggly Wiggly on University, I think." He starts laughing and trying to talk at the same time.

"What did he say? Somethin' about being 80 years old ... and about him bein' a Bread Man when what's-his-name, Jeff, was just a ... a daydream drippin' from his daddy's dick! That guy was none too happy. And I was thinkin', Jesus Frankie, I gotta come back here," he declares.

Bread Men love to tell stories, and Harold was no exception. He talked about all the bar fights he'd been in, and how he got a girl pregnant early on in life, blaming blind love and hormones, which is the reason most Bread Men are Bread Men.

"Are you married still?" I ask.

"I'm married, but not to the same gal. Maybe not for long though."

"What's going on, man? What makes you say that?" I ask quietly and watch him as he studies my face and then looks away.

After some pressing, he confesses that she kicked him out and that he slept in his car down the road from the depot last night before coming into work.

"It's freezing out," I announce. "You're stayin' at my place tonight. I need a ride home anyway."

15

There are three rules to being a Bread Man. They are:

1. Never call in sick.
2. Never call in sick.

These first two can't be stressed enough. When a guy calls in, it means Frankie has to run the route, and since Management can't be Union, he doesn't get paid for it. Frankie always gets out of running the route, but he has to jump through so many hoops that if you call in, he will kill you.

3. Mustaches are the only facial hair allowed.

For some reason, this rule applies to all Bread Men. Frankie, Walter, and Kim all have mustaches. The president of the company—mustache. Me, I have a beard. This wasn't an issue until Todd took over. He left a razor in my mailbox this morning at the depot with a note attached that said simply: LOVE TODD. Harold and I have just walked in, and Frankie's been waiting for us both.

"Did you see that fuckin' note Todd left you there Grizzly Adams? What do ya think that means?"

"I don't know. It means that Todd is gay?"

"No, it means you're gonna shave that beard, or I will. What do ya think Todd's gonna think if I can't get all my guys to obey the dress code?"

"Look Frankie, if I was baking the bread, I'd see the point; but it doesn't make any sense that you can't deliver bread with a beard. All Adams men have beards; it's part of my identity."

"It's the rules and we follow the rules or people die!" he yells.

Actually, we broke every rule but the first two. Everyone did. We smoked in the trucks, wore headphones while we drove, left stale loaves on the shelves, skipped accounts, sold old bread as new bread, took loaves home and sold them in greasy neighborhoods for cash, showed up late, and so on. We all knew that the only thing that could get you fired was not showing up to work. As long as Frankie didn't have to run the route, the rest was optional.

"Well, at least trim it for Christ's sake. And don't you go growin' a beard on me, Harold. The only reason I'm allowin' it is 'cause Todd went around me and asked Adams directly, that fuckin' control freak prick."

The depot falls silent for a second, until Frankie cuts through it. "What are you waitin' for? Load the fuckin' trucks."

I spend the next fourteen hours taking stale bread off the shelves and explaining to grocery store managers what happened the day before. Some laugh, some are pissed. When I arrive back home, I'm exhausted in every way, and sleep for the first time in a while. Before my eyes finally close, I wonder if Harold has anywhere to go tonight.

16

IT MUST BE AROUND TWO A.M. AND NATALIE HAS AWOKEN me after about an hour of drunkin' sleep.

"Do you keep everyone at arm's length?" I ask for some reason.

She doesn't respond. I listen to her breathe for a moment, and then I whisper, "Did I ever tell you the story of the bunny?"

"The story of the bunny?" whispers Natalie in return.

I pause to hear her breathe and start to breathe softly in unison with her, expanding my stomach, concentrating on my diaphragm, my hands crossed behind my head.

"Yeah, the story of the bunny. I was dog-sitting, playing Frisbee with my buddy's dog Lizzy. She's obsessed with the Frisbee. So, I knew somethin' was up when instead of chasing it down, she wandered in the grass in a circle, pawin' at the ground. A few seconds later, she had 'retrieved' a newly born baby bunny from out of the ground, and proudly laid it at my feet."

I just keep looking up at the ceiling, following one blade on the fan above, as it spins around and around and around. "The little guy was about seven inches long, with a full coat of hair, but young enough to still have his eyes closed. She had grabbed him really gently, but the little guy was so tender she tore thru both sides of his body, leavin' em' squirming on his side. I looked back at her, not mad. She was only doing what dogs do. I just kept looking at her. She was wagging her tail, but so slowly. She would sniff him and lick him and sit back down. She had no idea what she had done. So, I called my friend to ask if he had a shovel I could get too, thinking I'd flatten em'."

I take a long breath. "He told me that the garage door was locked, so I'd 'have to stomp it'. '*Stomp it*? Will that do it?' I asked. He said, 'That'll do it'. I turned off my cell phone and stared off into the window of the next house over. I remember there was a cat in the window. I had to put it out of its misery I told myself. And besides, I'm not a vegetarian. It would be hypocritical and cowardly to only be disturbed when it was me that had to do the killin'. I prayed. I asked God to forgive me and raised my foot. I looked again at Lizzy, then again at the bunny. I remember that the grass between them looked so green. I decided that if I was going to do it, I'd do it right. So ... I brought my foot down as hard as I could."

Natalie's' eyes widen as though she is doing it with me. Her hands rise up to the side of her face, her fingertips to her temples.

"The bunny must have just fed, 'cause milk shot out in every direction. It splashed all over my legs and on Lizzy, and the picnic table near the house. She looked up at me, head tilted, ears back. I lifted my foot to see. I had completely flattened him. There was no blood, only milk. He didn't make a sound, or she or whatever, but what was left of it was twitching and convulsing. I remember its mouth kept openin' and closin' like a goldfish or something. I took off my shirt and laid it on top of him, partly without thinking about it, and partly because I couldn't bear to look at him. I went to the back of the house and turned on the hose. I was wearing sandals, and my feet were covered in milk. I washed myself down and had this uncontrollable urge to dowse myself with water. I sprayed it over my head and chest, and again I started praying. Now mind you, I pray all the time, but this time was different. I had never killed anything before."

I took another deep breath. "I prayed to God to undo it. I didn't want the feeling still lingering in my gut. I thought of my father. I stuck my fingers down my throat and vomited. And here's the crazy part. I walked over to pick it up and felt around atop the shirt. Nothing. And I swear to God everything was as I left it. Lizzy was still sitting where she had been, the shirt was unmoved, the indent of a tiny bunny had been there staring at me, but no bunny. I stood there in awe … I mean the real meaning of the word. My head was buzzin', my eyes watering … I grabbed Lizzy and opened her mouth, looking for remnants of hair or flesh. Nothing. I checked the ground between her and where the shirt had been. Nothing. Maybe she grabbed it and hid it somewhere I thought. Then I remembered the milk. I looked all around the yard, thinking I'd find a milk trail to where she might have taken it. That's when I noticed there was no milk. None on the picnic table, none on the grass, none on Lizzy. I sat down in the grass and tried to think. I was dazed, you know? I considered that maybe I was dreaming and thought about trying to wake myself up. I even pinched myself. This is crazy, but it's true. I've never told anyone this, except my mom and dad and brother, but I thought maybe God had undone it.

"The reason I'm telling you this, the point I'm trying to make is I'm not willing to say I *know* what happened. I refuse to just say that the dog ate it. You know what I mean? Maybe that's why people think there are no miracles. Maybe they just dismiss what they consider impossible. Or maybe it's why people see Jesus in their toast. I don't know. Maybe there are no miracles. All I'm saying is for the first time in my life, I considered it.

"So, I called and told my parents I needed to talk. I had them put me on speakerphone and told them the story. My mom yelled, 'What did you do to these boys?' and my dad said, 'Nothing'."

Natalie just stared, not saying a word.

"You know how if you just look at one blade you can see it spinning so clearly?" I ask and watch her eyes move to the ceiling fan, but her eyes are not circling.

"You're the only person I know who talks about God," she whispers.

"Well, by God I just mean that thing no one can name … or really talk about or write about. I'm not a literalist when it comes to God. All I know is that, at some point, something came out of nothing. Even scientists can't explain where the gasses and so on came from to create the Big Bang. The center of our galaxy is a black hole, so what is its opposite? I think if there is a language we can use to explain God, it's science. But science can't tell us why, only how. And that start point isn't all that much more impressive than 'let there be light', ya know? Religion pretends to know. I know that. I don't know. I just find it terribly interesting. What do you talk about with your friends?"

"Science," she said.

I had awoken to find her in my bed. I always left my door unlocked and she had let herself in, taken off her clothes and crawled into bed with me. We made love for the last time at three in the morning, and I went to work exhausted in every possible way. It was day three of Harold's training, and the snow was beginning to melt. It wasn't that spring was on its way. It was just warming up for a spell.

17

LATER THAT MORNING, I SAT ON THE BUMPER OF A BREAD truck and tried to sip my coffee.

"Jesus Christ, boy, did you just come from the bar or what? You gotta start getting some sleep. I don't wanna get a call sayin' you drove my truck into a fuckin' bridge embankment."

"He's probably been up all night fuckin'," grins Walter.

Frankie begins to laugh. "Is that right, boy—with this Natalie broad?"

"I have to break it off with her," I say.

"What's that, Junior?"

This is the first time I said it aloud, and I didn't even notice that I had.

"You wait there, boy; ol' Frankie's got somethin' for ya."

Frankie walks to the front of the depot and opens the garage door. A minute later he comes squealing into the garage in the company van, the windows down, and some country song blaring. At the chorus, some fake cowboy is asking his love if she has come to save him.

Frankie hops out and starts singing along, the music blaring as he opens the door. He's screaming "are you the one who's come to save me" over and over. I force a smile for the first time in a long time and start loading my truck.

PART 2

18

My father called me the next day to tell me he had cancer. It was Christmas Eve. My mom had gone to D.C. to spend Christmas with my brother and sister-in-law, and I was going to work all week. He told me not to worry, but his voice said this might be my last Christmas with him.

"When did you find out?" I ask softly. It was the only thing I could think to say.

"They called me yesterday."

I was sitting in the truck behind my first account. The snow was really coming down, huge flakes melting quietly as they hit the windshield. I started to tap the steering wheel with my hand, and there was a long pause.

"What kind is it?"

"I have skin cancer. The VA says I have the Agent Orange." Again, a long pause. He tried to laugh and told me not to worry.

"I'm coming home right now," I tell him.

I expected him to reassure me and to tell me not to worry again. Instead, silence.

I thought of the bunny. I asked God to undo it and told my father I loved him.

"I love you too," he said.

"I'm gonna throw all my bread in this store. I'll be home as soon as possible. O.K.?"

"O.K." he replied.

19

After dumping all the bread, I called Natalie. She agreed to meet me before she started work.

"I'm sorry I can't be here right now" is how I started it on a bench next to the lake in the park. It was sunrise, and even if I hadn't gotten the news about my father, I was going to say what I had to say.

"What is it exactly?" she whispered.

"If I knew what to call it, I'd know how to fix it. I don't know. I guess, I don't feel human. Kinda like a camera or something. I don't know where I've gone. I just know I don't love you. And I'm leaving soon," I said coldly. I didn't mean for it to sound harsh, but also didn't care.

I stared out over the lake and listened to her sniffle. There were two geese floating in front of us. The sun was out and reflected off the water. She was so young. She listened to all my bullshit and, even now, she had no idea. I mean, I always said what I meant, but nothing I once meant made sense anymore.

I remember a dead fish next to the dock near where we sat. I remember there was little snow, except for the mounds where the snowplows had made little mountains that were now tiny brown ice patches. I remember that we later walked in circles around the neighborhood, completely lost on small house-filled roads, freezing on Christmas Eve. She once broke the silence with, "Isn't that beautiful?"

A two-seater bike with a father in front and a little girl sitting behind had just passed by.

"Yeah, if that little girl enjoys staring at her father's ass all day," was my response.

She whipped her head around and said, "You fucking freak pedophile."

She was livid. I was neutral. I wasn't even trying to break the ice really; it was simply the only thought that came to mind for some reason. I didn't say another word for some time.

I don't remember much of what she said, but this is all on my mind as I start to look for Frankie's number to call in sick.

20

"CAN'T HELP YOU ADAMS. I'M SICK. SICK OF GETTING fucked in the ass," mutters Frankie.

"Come on, man. I need it off. Can't you do the pulls tomorrow?"

"Where you at? What are we 'one-stop-droppin'-it' or what? Are we just putting all our bread in Woodman's, or did ya donate it to a homeless shelter? I just wanna know."

"Frankie, will you just listen to—"

"No, *you* listen. Let me explain something to you, O.K.? See, you'd make a shitty Marine. Did you know that? I got Todd up my ass callin' me on the phone sayin', 'Hey Frankie, how's one of your guys pull off a two-hour day the day before Christmas?' and I'm thinking to myself, gee, who's fuckin' me now? Is it Walter? No can't be Walter, he may be an asshole, but he wouldn't stab ol' Frankie in the back. And it can't be Harold, 'cause I'm with Harold. Must be Kim. Kim must be fuckin me, 'cause I know it ain't Adams. Adams would never do that after all I've done for him. Give him the best route in the depot, coverin' his fuckin' ass, keepin' shit from Todd, know what I mean? So, I think to myself, if I get to the depot and ol' Kimmy's still there, I'm gonna' string him up in the garage and fuckin' field dress him like a fuckin' deer. Then he tells me, 'No, no it's not Kim, it's the one you let do anything he wants, like have a beard and be a fuck-up'. You know I'm still coverin' your ass for fillin' up that fuckin' truck with gasoline? I got Todd asking me how come I send him a $500 dollar bill from Ronnie's for a fuckin' flush-out and refill of a whole goddamn tank of diesel. Adams! Shave that fuckin' beard. You look like a goddamn hippie. Has your father seen you lately?

"And what's this shit about 'I'm sick'? Bread Men don't get sick, Junior. Wrap your ass in a blanket, blast the heat, and drink whiskey all night till you sweat it out or pass out. Then get your ass in here and hit all your stores. Every fuckin' one of 'em! And tell all the managers that the shipping truck flipped on the way down today and that you're bringin' them their bread the day *of* Christmas, not because you're a huge fuck-up who likes to fuck people in the ass, but you're such a loyal vender, that your delivering *on* Christmas. Then I want you to go back out and do all your pulls. Oh, and you'll have to take everything in the front, 'cause Receiving is closed on Christmas. Got it? Good!"

"Can I explain ...?"

"No, I gotta call Todd back and get my ass chewed some more. That's all Frankie gets for Christmas. An ass-chewin'. If the world knew who I was, no one would fuck with me."

Click.

I lay my hands on my head for a moment and collect my thoughts. I'm about to do something I never thought I'd do to Frankie. I'm going to call Todd, and then I'm leaving for home.

21

When I get to my parents' house that afternoon, I find my father asleep in his recliner, an empty bowl resting on his stomach. His teeth are out and beside him on the tray table to his right, balanced on top of the landline phone. Next to that is his retirement gift from his last job at 3M: a gold ring with the tiniest collection of diamonds. He's still in his janitor's shirt, his cell phone in his right hand, the remote control in his left. He's 63, but life has made him look much older. For the first time in a long time it occurs to me that his hair is silver gray. His arms and hands are covered in liver spots. The skin of his calves stretches around varicose veins. His two big toenails are missing from boot rot. I picture him looking at me and remember that he has blue eyes.

He looks peaceful breathing in and out. It's the only time his face is relaxed. It makes me think of children for some reason. Vietnam has come to finish him off almost forty years later. I knew that it never left him, but it somehow seemed more real now.

I whisper his name, careful not to startle him. He usually wakes reaching for the invisible .45 strapped to his side, but sometimes grabs you and cocks his arm and fist. He doesn't respond, and I decide not to wake him. I lie down on the couch and think about Frankie. He rarely sees his kids. They're so young. I want to explain to them what war and fatherhood mean. I think of Natalie, her mother somewhere in the world, and wonder if a day goes by that she doesn't think of the family she left behind. All the Christmases and birthdays and Tuesdays she's missed. At this moment, I can't recall what I'm doing living in Wisconsin.

I fall asleep and dream of severed heads lined up in row upon row, stacked and stretching out like a panning camera, chanting something I imagine is Latin.

It's my father who startles me awake. He's smiling down at me, standing there in his underwear, his socks now pulled up. I think of an aqua blue T-shirt and a knife, and smile and say hello.

"Hi son! What are you doin' home? Don't you have to work?"

"I told ya I was comin' to see you. I got the day off tomorrow. Frankie's gonna cover for me."

"You didn't have to do that, son. Now I feel bad. How is old Frankie?"

"How the hell are ya? You look good," I say.

"Oh, I fell asleep in my damn chair. I don't know how your mother puts up with me. I never make it up to bed anymore."

"We gonna' go see a movie?" I ask.

"Yeah, if you want to. There's a good one at the dollar theater. Did you eat? Your mother made turkey and ham and mashed potatoes and left 'em in the fridge, I'm telling ya. Just help yourself. I gotta' piss somethin' fierce," he says as he starts walking to the bathroom. Waddling really, trying not to bend his knees.

I get up and go to the kitchen and fix myself a plate. When I come back down the stairs to the family room, he's back in his chair, struggling to put his teeth back in.

"Gotta' put my teeth back in," he tells me.

I just smile and sit on the couch.

"Anything good on?" I ask.

"I don't know, let's see."

He cycles through the guide, looking up over his bifocals, and we settle on a documentary about the life of Jesus. We don't talk much for the next several hours. We just watch TV and nibble turkey and crackers. I go outside to have a smoke and check my cell. I have no missed calls. I haven't heard from Frankie and try not to think about it.

When I get back, my father is asleep again, so I sneak a few shots of whiskey and have a beer. I switch the TV to CNN and check out what's happening in Iraq.

"That ain't no war,'" my dad says. He's woken up and I change the channel.

"No, go back. How did they die?"

"Another roadside bomb," I reply.

"Ah, I seen ambushes and what we used to call 'em was landmines before I re-enlisted. Most of the time we just drove around, ya know. What do they call em' now? Somethin' else."

"IEDs" I say.

"IDEs. Yeah. What the hell is an IDE?"

"IED. It stands for improvised explosive device. It's much more powerful than landmines. I heard that there is a type of truck that can withstand them, but the government doesn't want to pay. All we get is propaganda. I'm sure it's all much worse than the TV says. Especially Fox."

"Well, anyway, I requested to be put in the field for my second tour. You ain't seen nothin' till you been in the field. You remember that time I showed ya in the backyard what it was like?"

I force myself to laugh.

"You mean that time it was especially dark, and you stalked around to see if I could hear you."

"You remember that?" he smiles.

"I remember everything."

My father always talked about it. Vietnam.

I know that the first man he ever killed was up close. That he was "green and humpin' ammo" to the clip man, who then clipped the bullets on for the machine gunner, and three "gooks" came running out of a hut. I know that my father stood up, aiming, shooting the last guy in what he thought was the right shoulder, spinning him around. I know that he walked up to him through knee-high grass, aiming at his heart. That he pulled the rifle trigger. That he then looked down the barrel to see that his rifle was jammed, a shell sticking out. I know that he watched the man struggling to breathe, blood bubbles expanding and contracting from his chest. I know that it seemed like eternity before the others finished him off, all firing at once. I know my father thought of the man as married, with children. A man just like he would be, defending his country as he would. I know my father didn't eat for days. I know he killed more after that. I know that my father carries more baggage than any man I know. And I know that no matter how hard I tried to carry some for him, it was his double cross to bear.

I continue watching TV through the night. He's too tired to go to a movie I think to myself, and I'm too tired to sleep it turns out.

22

Christmas morning came hard. There was no snow, just gray, dead grass, matted down by strong winds and the previous snowfall. The trees looked burnt, and I imagine they would make my father think of firefights—the trees ripped of their foliage, splintered, and sparse.

There are birdhouses everywhere in the backyard. My father scratched his eye as a child, and his grandmother—who he thought was his mother until she told him the truth on her deathbed, right before he moved from the farm to the city to live with his real mother—bandaged both so he wouldn't move them while it healed. He told me that he just sat on the porch and listened to the birds sing. He was so grateful to have sight after that—and to be made to realize the beauty of the bird songs—that the rest he said was gravy. This he took with him to Vietnam ... and not even Vietnam could take it from him.

"Mornin', son! Did you eat yet?"

"I haven't got past the coffee."

"Come on, your mother left me a couple a' bucks. Let's go get some breakfast."

We arrive at the diner named Grandma's just a few turns away in the early morning. There are four TVs, all on swivels, all on FOX, covering the war. He's careful to sit where he can have his back facing away from the door, and we start on the coffee. He adds sweetener, looking up at the TV, and I try to concentrate on the menu. My eyes are heavy, and I'm still drunk on whiskey. The second the coffee hits my lips I start craving a cigarette.

"I'll be right back, Pop."

"Uh-huh," he says, not taking his eyes off the TV, and I step outside.

I check my phone again. Frankie still hasn't called. I think of calling my mother and start to hyperventilate. The universe is expanding. I am going to die one day. The sunflower literally moves and twists its stem so its face is always bent towards the sun. There are bones under this flesh, and my jaw will be the first to escape.

When I sit back down, it's all I can do to keep from bursting into tears.

"Your eyes look glassy," he says.

I want to say I haven't been sleeping, but don't. Instead, I just watch him watch me.

"You call your mother?"

"No. I will. It's early yet."

"You just don't know how much she loves you. She'd cut off her arm for you."

"I know, Pop," I say as I cross my arms and lean back, moving my eyes away from his, up to one of the TVs.

"I only pray that you find a gal as giving and loving as your mother. Come on now, talk to me. What's on your mind? I mean, you don't tell me nothin' no more. I know you, you sucker; you're a chip off the old block."

"I know. That's the problem," I say with a forced smile.

"How's your love life?"

"I don't have one."

"What about that one gal, what's her name? Aimee?"

"Natalie."

"Yeah, Natalie"

"I broke it off with her."

He looks down, shaking his head subtly, then looks up at me. His eyes are relaxed now and his hands are folded on the table in front of him.

"How's your feet?" I ask.

"The doc put me on morphine. So, good now," he laughs. "Everything happens for a reason. I applied for more disability, and if I got Agent Orange, that's even more money for your mother and yous'. So. You gotta look at the bright side. You can't spend your life feelin' depressed. A lotta what we got is the chemicals imbalance I'm discoverin'. Like your grandfather and your uncles and your grandmother. Your ma's mom. But the half of it is how you choose to look at life. If the cancer kills me ..."

He throws his hands up and shrugs his shoulders. "I thought I'd never make it out of Vietnam, now I get to listen to the birds singing every mornin', and enjoy my wife and family. Man, every day is a blessing. And if they tell me I got three months, I got three months.

"Ya never know son. Doctors have said that and then the person lives to a hundred. When it's your time, it's your time. I don't gotta do nothin' but die. The rest of it I choose to do. Hey man, I get to spend Christmas with my boy. What more could a man ask for?"

23

By the time I leave it's dark, and I don't feel like driving the two hours back to Madison. So, I head over to a high school buddy's house, smoke a bong and drink some beers. I tell him about my old man, and he starts talking about all the times my dad would come out when we were playing basketball in my front yard and preach to us about life and war.

"My dad never talks about it."

"What?" I ask, curious.

"Vietnam," he replies.

I don't respond. The weed has made me paranoid and I can't stop thinking about Frankie. I start to consider quitting, never showing up again. Maybe I'll just drive to California. I don't sleep at all, and head out somewhere around one a.m. The sun is coming up as I turn the corner heading toward the depot; there are no birds singing, and I take note of the company van in the parking lot.

24

As I walk in the front door of the depot, into the office that separates the front and the garage, my legs turn to jelly. My heart makes its way up my throat, and I start to dry-heave. The latter is partly due to the ten coffees and the pack of Lucky non-filters I consumed on the way here. I overhear what sounds like a debate about the existence of Bigfoot by Kim and a voice I don't recognize.

"They've got video footage; what more do you want?" demands the strange voice.

I gather myself as best I can, grab my order list, and walk into the garage to find Walter, Kim, some guy, and Todd. No Harold, and more importantly, no Frankie.

No one pays me much mind 'till Kim says, "Hey Buckwheat, this guy here thinks Bigfoot's real."

"Sasquatch," the stranger corrects.

I turn to Walter. "Where's Harold?"

"Harold doesn't work here anymore." he replies, then takes a bite out of a donut and a drag off of his cigarette. He does not elaborate.

Everyone is acting normal, or as normal as one can act with Todd around. No one offers any explanation as to what happened to Harold, or where Frankie is and, honestly, I'm so relieved, I don't say anything about it. I just start loading my truck as though nothing has happened.

"Well, you look like a smart guy—you know what you would call Bigfoot is real?"

I don't look up for fear of making eye contact with Todd, and out of the side of my mouth I say, "I don't know. Don't you think we would have found the remains of a Bigfoot by now? Or at least some droppings?"

It's clear from the long pause that he's never thought about it, but he's not about to lose the argument.

"You think people are gonna go camping if they know there are Bigfeet around? Park Rangers and whatnot help cover it up. Come on, man, use your head!"

"This is Brian," says Todd.

I look up and walk over to him to shake his hand. He's tall, 6'3 maybe, twice my girth, and he's missing some of his front teeth at the top. He has on what can only be called "Serial-Killer glasses". He's balding and obviously crazy. He'll make a perfect Bread Man.

"How was your Christmas?" asks Todd.

"Good. Thanks for the day off."

He doesn't respond, and we all go back to loading our trucks.

I light up a cigarette and Todd tells me I can't smoke in the depot. As I'm putting it out, I see Walter light a cigarette out of the corner of my eye. He's smiling and Todd looks up at him. Walter blows him a kiss, and Todd goes back to loading the truck. He doesn't say a word.

25

As I pull out of the depot, my head is spinning. The coffee is wearing off, and exhaustion is setting in. I light up another cigarette and crack the window just to stay awake. I look down and see that the tank is on "E". I start to say in my head, over and over, "Fill the tank with *diesel.*"

My body feels like liquid, and I start to cry. I cry all the way to the gas station, then again on the way to my first store. Nothing was done yesterday, but that's to be expected when you call in. I spend the next twelve hours apologizing for empty shelves and pleading with Store Managers not to take away my shelf space. I must look pitiful enough because I am forgiven everywhere I go. I make it through the day without hearing from Frankie and return to an empty depot. Instead of unloading my truck, I lie down in the back, and drift off to sleep.

26

Some time in my youth, preteen, I sat to the left of my father in a doctor's office, my brother to his right. He was leaning back, his hands resting on his stomach, mouth open, sleeping. My father could sleep anywhere. He once took a nap in his foxhole in the middle of a two-day firefight while being shelled and shot at, a dead "gook covered in maggots" just five feet away, next to what was left of a tree.

Since then, he's caught his sleep in small broken increments. When the nurse approached saying his name, I absently tapped him on the thigh. The next thing I saw was the back of his left hand and forearm crossing my nose. Through the tears I saw that, at the same time, he was grabbing my brother, his right hand grasping my brothers' shirt in the largest fist I have ever seen then or since—and, all in one motion, bringing the left back around, fist still clenched, and pausing inches away from my brothers' Coke-bottle glasses. I remember the nurse slowly inching back in terror as I tried to explain to her that it was my fault for waking him so abruptly. She did not seem to understand. It was one of those firsts that I would experience over and over again.

Like when I went to dinner with my friend's family in the second grade and was surprised when he responded to my legitimate concern with, "Why would we wait for a booth in the back?"

"So, your dad can watch the door," I responded.

Or the time in the sixth grade when my friend's father was teaching him how to box.

"Will you teach me how to box, Dad?" I recall asking that day.

"Nothin's worth fightin' for unless it's worth dyin' for. And if you decide it's worth dyin' for, then kill the son of a bitch. I don't need to teach you how to kill. You were born knowing how."

All these things I recognized in Frankie. The frazzled wide-eyed look in his eyes. The dark circles from the short glimpses of rest. I could see the fighting he'd done in his eyes when they looked out from behind a cigarette. It was in the way he hurriedly did everything as though it was his last chance to do it. I heard it in his voice when he'd call to tell me about an accident he had passed on his way home, or the accident he saw coming and was calling to keep me posted on. He would even tell me straight out at times over a beer down the street after work. He'd always order two at the same time when he arrived, slam them both down, and order a third to sip. Then things like, "Nine Marines died that day, because I didn't supply them with cover" would come out of his mouth.

Or, "I was in Desert Storm and Desert Shield, and the politicians wouldn't let us finish the job in either of 'em. If they'd let us deal with 'em then, we wouldn't have to be there now. But the fuckin' Liberals see one dead baby, and then we gotta leave. Now look how many dead babies there are, boy. I say drop the bomb on 'em."

He would say these things as though he were still there, still trying not to look. Telling himself he must accept it like a good Marine. This is where Frankie and my father differed. Neither of them trusted the government. Neither of them felt taken care of or appreciated by America. But Frankie was still a Marine.

"Once a Marine, always a Marine," he would say.

I once asked him what he would do if the country had been hijacked by hidden forces, the President and all the President's men mere puppets. Would he feel the same about America no matter who was in charge?

His reply: "I'd follow orders."

My father wanted to turn his rifle on every Congressman and Senator when he got home from Vietnam.

They had "killed the Good King, and 'Ask not what your country can do for you, but what *you* can do for your country' had died with Him," he said one morning while I was eating Lucky Charms.

He would never follow orders again. He was more of a preacher now than a soldier. Though my brother and I often joke about being raised in bootcamp, it was more like the seminary for me. The first and last thing my father read from front to back was the *New Testament*. It kept him company through Vietnam, and he came to the conclusion that all was God, and anyone trying to name it either wanted your money, your soul or both. When the Catholic Church said they wouldn't marry him and my mom in front of the altar unless she converted, he said, "You mean to tell me I can't marry the woman I love in front of the eyes of God?

"Yes," confirmed the priest.

My father's reply: "Then I guess God don't live here no more."

That day he started the process to convert to my mother's' religion: Eastern Orthodox. They married shortly after.

He gave me his copy of *The Bible* to read when I was thirteen. At first, I just read what he had underlined, then found myself rereading it and rereading it. Then I moved on to Buddhism and Dream Time, and all the things that rippled out. Mitakuye Oyasin and Ala and so on.

I once as a child asked my father, "Do you think you'd still be a Christian if you were raised in Tibet, Pop?"

"Yeah," he replied. "But I'd call him Buddha or whatever."

Frankie was Irish Catholic and that was that. Before every shot we'd take, he'd recite a toast, a monologue about being a watchman at the gates of Ireland, how lonely it was, wifeless, childless, but a guardian of all wives and all children. This was how he learned to deal with the loss of his family, and the country that seemed to turn its back on him. This is why he would treat me like a son. The only man I would betray Frankie for is my Father.

I thought of all these things as I held the phone in my hand when I awoke in the back of a bread truck. I had to make myself think of nothing to get up the nerve to call Frankie.

27

RING ... RING.

"Adams!" he answers.

"Frankie? What the hell's goin' on? Don't tell me I got you fired."

"No boy, I got M.S."

Every time Frankie had to run a route, something would happen to him so that he couldn't. Either a court date over child support, or surgery, and so on. Todd knew this, and Frankie had just developed Multiple Sclerosis the night I called in sick. I feel terrible, but I don't believe him, and feign concern, hoping the conversation doesn't turn into an ass-chewing.

"You know, boy, you're just like my thirteen year-old, figurin' out clever ways to fuck me over. Only at least you don't involve that cunt of a wife of mine."

"I'm so sorry Frankie, but my dad is sick."

"Yeah, we're all sick. I got M.S., boy. And you didn't do nothin' I wouldn't a done. Let Todd run the fuckin' route, let's you and me go to the bar and drink our faces off. Oh, and if you ever stab me in the back again, I'll cut your dick off and feed you to the pigs."

"I know Frankie, I know. I'm sorry."

"Yeah. We're all sorry, Junior. We're all fuckin' sorry as hell. You know that prick Todd doesn't believe me? He told me I probably know the doctor."

I said, "Yeah, he stood up in my wedding as a matter of fact, and I don't think he'd appreciate you insinuating that he's betraying his Hippocratic Oath. You're not doin' that are you Todd?'"

He starts to laugh—three loud ha-ha-has.

"Then I called HR and reported Todd for badgerin' me after I just found out I got M.S. and threatenin' my job. That motherfucker thinks he's smart. Well, who's on the route with Brian? That's all I wanna know, boy! Who's on the route? Oh yeah, Todd's on the route!" He starts to laugh again, this time a long hiss through blackened lungs. Frankie's wasted.

"Oh, you know about Brian? What happened to Harold?" I ask.

"Harold went to work for Wonder Bread. Yeah, nice fuckin' hire Todd. You think I didn't see that comin', boy. Well, I ain't trainin' another one of his fuck-ups. I been dyin' since the day I was born, and it's about time I started livin', ya know what I mean?"

"Did you see it comin'?" I question.

"What?" he asks, confused.

"The M.S.?"

"Oh no. It can take years for the symptoms to show up. They gotta run some more tests and whatnot—I gotta go back again tomorrow.

"Well, boy, I'd love to talk more, but I'm watchin' a porno right now, so ah, I'll call you tomorrow and let you know what the doctor says since you're the only one who gives a fuck about old Frankie. Say hi to Todd for me."

I hear him laughing as he hangs up the phone. He didn't threaten to kill me. Not exactly anyway. I am more relieved than is imaginable. That only lasts for a moment, however, and my thoughts drift back to cancer.

PART 3

28

CAN·CER (K N S R)

n. 1.

a. Any of various malignant neoplasms characterized by the proliferation of anaplastic cells that tend to invade surrounding tissue and metastasize to new body sites.

b. The pathological condition characterized by such growths.

2. A pernicious, spreading evil: A cancer of distrust spread throughout the depot.

Can·cer (k n s r)

n. In all senses also called Crab.

1. A constellation in the Northern Hemisphere near Leo and Gemini.

a. The fourth sign of the zodiac in astrology.

b. One who is born under this sign.

Cancer (k n s r)

A Closer Look: The human immune system often fights off stray cancer cells just as it does bacteria and viruses. However, when cancer cells establish themselves in the body with their own blood supply and begin replicating out of control, cancer becomes a threatening neoplasm, or tumor. It takes a minimum of one billion cancer cells for a neoplasm to be detectable by conventional radiology and physical examinations.

I am so tired. I'm sitting by the window in my efficiency reading Hemingway's *The Garden of Eden,* sipping Scotch and drinking Guinness, and chain smoking homemade cigarettes—weed papers and the leftover tobacco from an old ashtray— because it's all I have the energy for.

Todd has been in every morning for a week, and if that's not enough stress, today is New Year's Eve. I had a truck full of buns on top of my normal order; all told, a twelve-hour day. I have to get up early tomorrow to "do the pulls". (On Sundays, I go to the stores and restock the shelves; that's what is known as doing pulls). I'll probably head to the bar after work though. I've been going to the bar with Todd and Brian every day, picking Todd's brain, trying to convince him that Frankie is a good boss. He sure makes a shitty Mormon. I've never seen anyone drink so much. And he has the sexual appetite of a teenager. Brian's divorced, with a daughter. She was born both a boy and a girl, and as he put it, "Now her intestines are hangin' outta' her twat." He said this as he dangled and wiggled two fingers at me.

"She's gotta have another surgery Monday. What am I gonna say if she dies? I was busy deliverin' bread?"

"Just have Todd run the route," I said.

"Frankie's bein' a prick sayin' Todd can't run the route alone."

Todd started as a Bread Man. He had apparently showed up the first day in a suit, thinking he was a "Bread Salesman". I can't imagine what they must have said to him. But he was aggressive. He rose up the ladder quickly.

Frankie's been in the bread business for almost twenty years. He started as a baker in the warehouse in high school. How he ended up the manager of the least-grossing depot in the Midwest after being a Marine for ten years, a cop for ten, and somehow a bread man for twenty years, I never figured out.

Frankie once asked me to guess his age. "Fifty-six," I said, thinking of all he'd said that he'd done in his life.

"I'm thirty-fuckin'-nine, Junior," he declared in all seriousness with fire in his eyes.

The mind has wandered. I realize that I haven't been reading at all, that my eyes have just been skimming the page. The words all at once begin to jump out at me, and I read *Eden* in peace for a few hours before I run across the street to buy another six-pack from the taco place. I need something to wash down the fifth of Glenfiddich and the four-pack of Guinness I decide. The night is warm, the pavement wet and slick. The slush grunts it's mush as cars go by, the timing and syncopation growing more rhythmic with every second.

I cross the street and see Natalie inside. She's sitting at a table alone, headphones on her ears, her nose in a textbook. She does not look up. I stare at her for a moment or two. At this moment I love her with all my heart, but I know not to trust it. I can't trust myself. My eyes start to water, and I begin to sob.

I run back across the street and head into my apartment building. It smells like fall. My worn shoes squeak as I walk down the hall and straight out the back towards the lake. I become conscious of the sound of my breathing. It's speeding up. A martini comes to mind; so, I wipe my eyes, walk around front, and head into the little Italian place next to my apartment. The owner is behind the bar, and we say our hellos.

"You look tired," he states. "I know. I was a Bread Man for many years." He encourages me to find a new line of employment, as he always does.

"Extra dry martini. Grey Goose," I say.

"O.K." I'm in no mood to talk about work or career decisions, and the couple at the table nearest the bar becomes of interest to me. They look to be in their late 70s. He is dressed in a sports coat and dress pants, she in a modest gown. They reek of love. I ask if it's their anniversary and sit down to chat with them while they eat.

"What's the secret?" I ask.

"Well, he pretty much does whatever I say," she smiles.

He laughs and says, "Now that's true. I've learned not to argue."

They are so soft to one another: soft-spoken, slow-moving, patient, kind. I start to wonder if people of their generation were always like that, even when they were young, or if it's something that comes with age—growing together with the common commitment that, no matter what, one will not turn his or her back on the other.

The owner comes out from behind the bar and nervously asks me if I was invited to sit down.

"Yes," I say without thinking.

"Yes," the woman graciously says and smiles at me.

"Oh. I see. Forgive me for interrupting," he states with a rueful smile.

"How did you know? I'm sorry, is it your anniversary? That's why I sat down ... is *love* real?" I ask them, my gaze darting back and forth between their eyes.

He starts to speak, looking uneasy, prefacing his story with a year I don't pay attention to. Cancer has come back to me. "My father won't get any more moments," I think aloud.

"What's that, dear?" she asks.

God is in my head. Suddenly, I'm standing. She looks frightened and turns to her husband as she tries to comfort me. She touches my elbow cautiously and asks what's wrong.

All my words are slurred between gasps of breath. I'm almost drooling when the owner grabs me by the arm and starts to escort me out. Love is in my head again, and I wish it would stop.

29

I WAKE TO FIND THE SUN BEHIND THE CLOUDS. IT SNOWED all night and the winds have made three or four feet drifts in places. It's Sunday, New Year's Day, and I have to do pulls. I arrive at the first store, coffee and cigarette in hand, and the wind tells me to hurry up and get inside.

I go straight to the back. It's Woodman's, our biggest account, and they go through so much bread, there's no point in checking the shelves. As I'm wheeling out two stacks of buns, I run into Marie, the bakery manager.

"Good morning ..." I sing. "Good morning, beautiful Marie." I'm doing Bing Crosby.

She smiles from ear-to-ear and says good morning. Marie hates Frankie. She hates anything that has to do with our company, except me. We hit it off right away. I discovered if I just kept talking, she didn't have time to bitch at me. And if I could get her to laugh, it was all the better: a win-win.

"Oh, Marie, I woke this morning feelin' like the letter Q. Oh, my back. Will you stock my bread for me?" I smile.

"Yeah right," she responds and then mouths the words "fuck you".

I laugh out loud and ask her, "Why must you torture me like this

Marie? Can't you see I love you? I still remember when it was my name that passed through your lips, as soft as newborn-baby dreams. Kiss me Marie. Kiss me now!" I feign lunging at her, and she gets the belly laughter.

I watch her stomach flex in and out and think to myself how strange laughter is. The body convulses, gasping for breaths, all because we have consciousness, and these immaculate grunts we call language can actually make the body convulse. It's magic to me.

I go about stocking and am done in less than an hour. I decide to skip all the small stores, like I always do on Sundays. Tomorrow, I'll bitch about the Pull Guy to the Store Managers. They'll never know it's me who is screwing them, and I get paid either way. I'm Union. Fuck 'em. It's not 'till I get home and see the empty bottle and cans that I remember what had happened the night before.

30

MONDAY IS MONDAY. ALL THE BREAD YOU DIDN'T SELL, stale on the shelf, more money out then in, working not only for free but paying them back for the false hopes that a display in the front of the store needed three trays of back stock, only to find them all sitting there next to the display in the backroom. Who can blame them? No one wanted Butternut. It was a Brown Berry area, then all the others: Wonder Bread, Sarah Lee, and Pepperidge Farms. Brown Berry and Pepperidge Farms Bread Men owned their own routes, made six figures. Butternut was David with no stone.

It makes me think of my brother and childhood; it was us against the world. More him against the world really, as I don't have a confrontational bone in my body. It was my job to hold his glasses. I remember, one day, on the bus when we were young—I was ten, so he must have been twelve or thirteen—when the boy sitting behind us kept gleeking on the back of my brother's neck and head. His spit was wiped each time by my brother's hand as I sat next to him. He'd just calmly wipe off the spit and keep looking straight ahead. It was "a big kid", so I did nothing, said nothing, but my heart sank every time he did it, every time I heard his friends laughing and bantering back and forth.

When the bus pulled up to the school and we all stood, I followed my brother, who was careful to wait until the kids behind us walked past. He followed them and I followed him, as always. Right before we got to the front of the bus, he simply turned to me, took off his glasses and handed them to me, not saying a word. As soon as he stepped off the bus, he grabbed the kid from behind by the hair, kicked the back of his knee in and violently slammed his head against the concrete as the boy screamed, his legs caught under him like a pretzel. He slammed his head three or four times, the blood rushing out of his head in a slowly expanding pool as he lay there crying. I just watched and held his glasses.

31

My father once spoke to me of a woman named Francis. She was his fiancée three times while he was away in Vietnam, the last time just three weeks before he met my mother. I feel guilty bringing her up before I really talk about my mother, but if I spend more than a second on Mom, all turns to dribble. Francis I can handle. She was some woman who sent my father care packages with baseball cards and sardines while he was in Vietnam. My father didn't care much for baseball, but the sardines he learned to love. He would hold one between his teeth while "humpin'" hills in the jungle, gently squeezing out the moisture, something to pace himself on as he humped up hills and valleys, the foliage too thick to walk through without the aid of a machete, through the thick clouds of mosquitoes and fear.

He imagined that back home there were fast cars with the tops down, summer nights, and Christmas lights and soda pop, but it was all fantasy. The truth is my father was made for my mother, and he wouldn't find this out until the well of his heart was properly dug out, leaving enough space to hold the love she would give him.

Me, I was just two years abstinent when I met Natalie. And then wham, left hook, uppercut, combination overhand right, overhand left, right cross, left cross, finish him! I still couldn't help but be aware that I didn't know what it was like "to know". My father just seemed "to know". My mom was the one, and that was that. Francis was a memory tied to sardines and baseball cards, just as Natalie was a memory tied to bread and coffee—that and the dream of marriage.

32

I ARRIVE AT THE DEPOT AROUND SIX A.M., ABOUT THREE hours late, and everyone is gone. I load my truck, down three cups of coffee and a dozen or so cigarettes, eat some doughnuts I'm supposed to deliver, and my gut starts rotting. I'm so behind that I might as well take a shit before I go, I think to myself. It's too late before I realize that there's no toilet paper. Frankie still hasn't been in to order it, or do anything else for that matter, so I use a ton of paper towels, pissed off because it scratches so damn much, and I'm off to charge through my day.

I cut every corner imaginable. I "face up" stores that don't need much bread; that is, instead of delivering there, I just straighten the shelves, and away I go. I skip some of the smaller stores, and I skip adding point-of-sale stickers and so on. All told, I make it to my last stop with fifteen minutes to spare before Receiving closes. So, I'm in a better mood when I make it back to the depot before dark.

My phone has been ringing non-stop for the past three hours. It was a Madison number, but I didn't recognize it. I remember that it's shut off and turn it back on as I hop out of the truck. Water splashes on my pants when I hit the ground. I don't have time to think much of it, as my phone is already ringing again.

"Hello!" I yell, annoyed.

"Adams, you're alive!"

It's Brian.

"Just callin' to make sure you're O.K.," he says.

"Yeah, I just overslept."

"Overslept? No, I mean I'm makin' sure Frankie didn't kill you."

"You saw Frankie today? How's he doin'?" I ask excitedly.

"You mean, you don't know? Where are you?"

"I'm at the depot."

He shouts, "Get the hell outta there!"

Panic sets in. The words "Frankie", "kill", and "get the hell outta there" were just uttered, so I don't ask any questions. I run violently, arms flailing as I head for the door. That's when I see Frankie in the window. He's on his way in, and he looks livid.

I hang up on Brian and try to think. Maybe he hasn't seen me. I run into the garage, and the door opens, followed by a loud howl of, "Adams!"

Fuck, I've been spotted. I wrack my brain, trying to think of what I have done. Does he know I was late? Was he still pissed about me calling in? I peek my head through the door.

"Hey Frankie," I smile.

He just stands there, looking at me. I notice his pants are wet up past the ankle.

"What happened to your pants?" I ask casually.

Again, he just stares. Slowly, he tilts his head to the side like a confused dog, and asks, "Do you hate me, boy?"

"What ...?"

"Do. You. Hate me?"

"No Frankie, what's—"

"I know I can lose my temper sometimes, and sometimes maybe I'm even a little bit of a prick, but don't I try, boy? I *try*, right?"

"Well, yeah."

"And what do I get in return?"

I assume that he's just going to interrupt me again, so I wait silently. He says nothing.

"Well Frankie, I don't—"

"I'll tell you what I get. I get fucked in the ass. You know. I just get outta the hospital, thanks for visitin' me by the way, and I say to myself, I think I'll go to the depot and see my favorite Bread Man. Know what I mean?

And what do I find when I get here?"

Again, there's a pause. I take note that I'm standing perfectly still, afraid to move, like one would do if they stumbled upon a vicious stray dog. It feels like my heart is about to explode, and I notice sweat rolling down my forehead. When I move to wipe it Frankie blurts out, "I find four assholes, Todd included, with their trucks parked in the parking lot, each one of 'em with a bigger shit-eatin' grin than the next! You know why they're smilen', boy? They're smilen' because they're not the ones that are gonna have to spend the next five hours moppin' up the shit in the depot. Now when I say shit, I mean shit, human fucking feces. You stuffed paper towel down the fuckin' toilet and left the goddamn depot to turn into your shit farm."

"I clogged the toilet?"

"No, you clogged the whole goddamn drain, and shit backed up in the garage up to my fuckin' eyes, boy! I just spent my first day back knee-deep in your shit, cause Todd's too goddamn lazy to buy toilet paper for the depot while I'm away. You know I can still smell it, Junior. The smell of your shit is stuck in my fuckin' nose."

"Frankie, I—"

"Not a word, Adams. Not a fuckin' word. What are you gonna say? What can you possibly say that will undo the fact that I spent all morning and afternoon in my brand new goddamn boots moppin' up Bread Man shit? Now, if you'll excuse me, I'm gonna go home and douse myself with whiskey and light a match and jump in the fucking river."

Frankie turns and marches out. It *is* good to have him back.

EPILOGUE

ONCE BRIAN WAS TRAINED, THINGS PRETTY MUCH WENT back to normal, except that Todd was around more often. He would pop in unexpectedly, trying to catch Frankie screwing up. It was a game of cat and mouse.

Frankie would try and get away with doing nothing, while Todd was trying to catch Frankie doing nothing. It was comical really, except for the fact that Frankie's job was on the line of course. But you had to give him credit. He had Todd doing his job for him, because Frankie wouldn't quit, and he made it his job to screw up everything Todd asked him to do. The world was his oyster, and he was making lemonade out of Todd. That is until about two weeks after I quit, planning to move back to Illinois.

One day, for reasons no one is quite sure of, Frankie said to Todd, "Why do I even get up in the morning, Todd? Why don't you call whoever's dick you gotta suck to get permission to fire me, and fire me?"

Todd did just that.

"Can you believe that, boy? He actually called me back and said he got permission. So I says' to him, 'you must suck a mean dick'," Frankie told me on the phone.

"What are you gonna do now?" I asked.

"I'm gonna sit by the river and drink my face off. I should be butt-naked and howlin' at the moon by eight o'clock"

They had cut all the cancer spots out of Dad's arms and legs, but one spot was deeper than the others, a place they were worried went to the bone. In that case, it would spell the end, and we waited anxiously as we were assured, time and time again, that this time they would get all of the cancer.

Natalie floated through my mind every now and again, and winter melted into spring. I would take long walks around the lake in the park behind my apartment. I'd admire the magic of rebirth everywhere I looked—in the buds on the trees, the birds building nests, the bees humming by, and the sweet smells of the Midwest. It would still snow and frost every now and again, the geese retreating to the center of the lake where it would not freeze, their underbellies exposed as they sat upright on the ice, shape-shifting into little penguins—but all in a spring like I remembered from childhood.

I started feeding the birds in the backyard, and even made friends with a squirrel. I'd spot a bunny every now and again through my window, but they never came around when I was in the yard. Word must have spread through the "bunny village".

My memory would often go back to the Italian restaurant, the words "my father won't get any more moments" rocking back and forth as though in a cradle, and I was trying to get them to sleep. But there wasn't much sleep going on at all. There was too much beauty everywhere, too much Sun and Love and God. I considered becoming a writer and thought to myself: why not do it while you're young? Do something while you are alive, before you get cancer or become so fucked up that you start faking you have M.S.

Frankie and I haven't talked since. He called and left me a message to share with Dad on Veterans Day. It would be the last time that I would ever hear from him. It was a poem he had written titled

"A Soldier's Story".

Lord, take my soul.

Make me whole again.
I've blown my top, I won't wake up.
They've called me fatty
And coward. And queer. And dead.
I drank their acid and concealed it.
Because I know the truth,
As simple as shaving soap.
That I will go to fight and die.
So that my Love may live.

Dear reader,

We hope you enjoyed reading *Memoirs Of A Bread Man*. Please take a moment to leave a review in Amazon, even if it's a short one. Your opinion is important to us.

Discover more books by Justin John Scheck at https://www.nextchapter.pub/authors/justin-john-scheck

Want to know when one of our books is free or discounted for Kindle? Join the newsletter at http://eepurl.com/bqqB3H

Best regards,

Justin John Scheck and the Next Chapter Team

YOU MIGHT ALSO LIKE

You might also like:
The Patriot Joe Morton by Michael DeVault

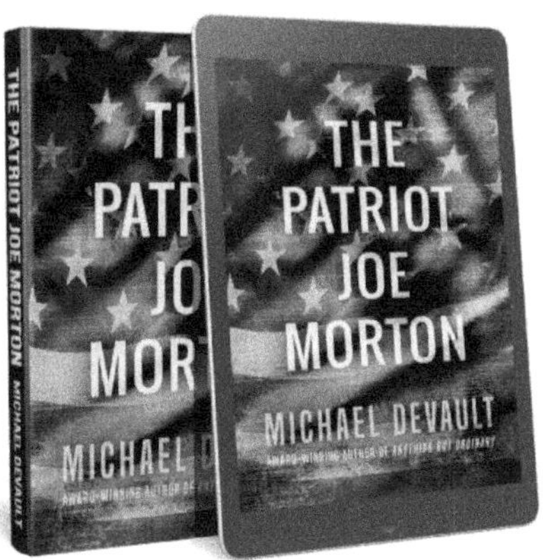

To read the first chapter for free, please head to:
https://www.nextchapter.pub/books/the-patriot-joe-morton

Lightning Source UK Ltd.
Milton Keynes UK
UKHW010954280820
368951UK00004B/150

9 781715 365912